GREETINGS WALLY-WATCHERS!

IT'S NEARLY CHRISTMAS! WE'VE POSTED OUR WISH LISTS TO SANTA – I HOPE THEY ARRIVE IN TIME!

JOIN ME, WOOF, WENDA, WIZARD WHITEBEARD AND ODLAW IN THIS MAGICAL WINTER WONDERLAND. THERE ARE LOTS OF SANTAS FOR YOU TO MEET, BUT LOOK OUT FOR THE REAL ONE – HE'S THE ONLY SANTA MISSING A BOOT. CAN YOU HELP HIM FIND IT BEFORE HIS TOES TURN TO ICICLES? BRRR-ILLIANT!

WHILE YOU SEARCH, USE THE STICKERS IN THE MIDDLE OF THE BOOK TO SOLVE THE SUPER-COOL PUZZLES (EACH ONE HAS ITS OWN SET!) THEN CREATE A DAZZLING SCENE AT THE END. WOW!

Wally

DANCING ON ICE

Stick the stickers on top of the matching silhouettes to complete the scene.

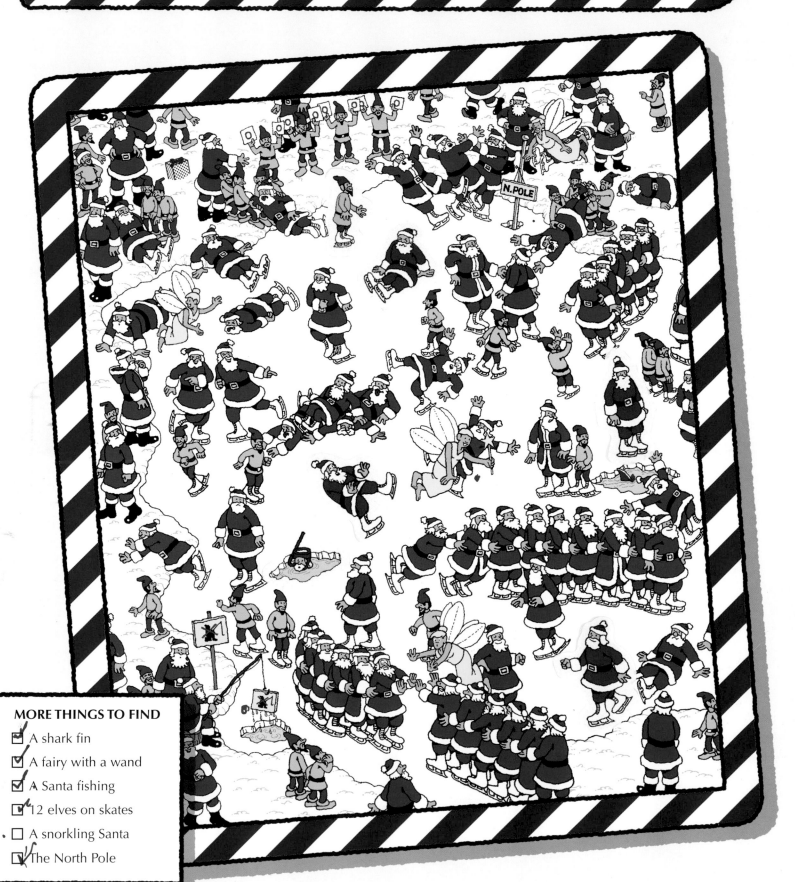

MORE THINGS TO FIND

- ☑ A shark fin
- ☑ A fairy with a wand
- ☑ A Santa fishing
- ☑ 12 elves on skates
- ☐ A snorkling Santa
- ☑ The North Pole

SANTA'S SACK RACE MAZE

Place the elf stickers on the correct coloured squares. Then find each Santa a way to the finish line by passing elves holding presents that match the red or blue colour of their sack.

START

START

FINISH

MORE THINGS TO DO

* Which Santa passes the most presents on their route?

* Find two presents with starry wrapping paper.

DEAR SANTA

Read the wish lists to Santa from Wally and his friends. Can you guess who the senders are and the presents they wished for, and stick down the correct stickers?

Bow-Wow, Santa,
I'm always hungry
for something to dig
up or chase! It would
be a real treat to
get another of
my favourite
things to
chew on!

Santa

The Worksh

DEAR CLAUS, OLD CHAP,
I'M CATCHING A
CHILL FROM WALKING
BAREFOOT IN THE
SNOW! IT WOULD
BE MAGICAL IF YOU
COULD CONJURE UP
SOMETHING
TO KEEP MY
FEET WARM.

SANTA

THE WORKSHOP

THE NORTH POLE

DEAR SANTA, SIR,
CAN YOU DELIVER ME
A JOKE PRESENT SO I
CAN HAVE SOME SNEAKY
FUN? I LIKE THINGS
THAT ARE
CREEPY
AND
CRAWLY.

SANTA

THE WORKSHOP

THE NORTH POLE

DEAR FATHER CHRISTMAS,
I LOVE ARTS AND CRAFTS!
PLEASE CAN I HAVE A KIT
TO MAKE SOME JOLLY
PAPER CHAINS TO
HANG UP?

SANTA

THE WORKSHOP

Dear Mr Claus,
A chilled, sweet
and tasty gift with
extra sprinkles for
me, please!
Anything to
keep
me cool!

Santa

The Workshop

The North Pole

HI THERE, SANTA,
I CAN'T WAIT FOR MY
NEXT ADVENTURE!
DO YOU HAVE A GIFT
THAT MIGHT HELP
ME DECIDE
WHERE TO
TRAVEL TO?

SANTA

THE WORKSHOP

THE

MORE THINGS TO DO

★ Write your own letter to Santa. Be sure to leave it where he'll find it, with a mince pie!

★ Make Christmas cards to send to your family and friends. Fold a piece of paper or card in half; draw a picture on the front or use spare decorations such as tinsel or leftover stickers to decorate; then write your festive message inside.

WENDA'S CLEVER CLOGS QUIZ

Complete Wenda's quiz by placing a tick sticker in the box next to each correct answer.

Where in the world is the North Pole?
- ☑ The Arctic
- ☐ The Alps
- ☑ The Atlantic

What is a baby reindeer called?
- ☐ Pup
- ☐ Cub
- ☑ Calf

How many days are in December?
- ☐ 29 days
- ☐ 30 days
- ☑ 31 days

Evergreen trees are:
- ☑ Green all year round
- ☑ Never green
- ☐ Only green in winter

Polar bears can…
- ☐ Dance
- ☐ Shake hands
- ☑ Swim

What is a toboggan?
- ☐ An arrow
- ☑ A sledge
- ☐ A cake

Which is the correct song title?
- ☑ Jingle Bells
- ☐ Jingle Toes
- ☐ Jingle Hips

How many points does a snowflake have?
- ☐ 5
- ☑ 6
- ☐ 7

HOME SWEET HOME

Decorate the Christmas tree with stickers to make it look jolly and bright!

MORE THINGS TO FIND

Did you hang any of these on your tree?

☐ Two drums

☐ A polar bear

☐ A robin

☐ Two red baubles

☐ A gingerbread man

☐ A penguin

☐ Ten bells

ALL WRAPPED UP!

Finish these puzzles! The same item can only appear once in every row, once in every column and once in every group of four squares. Game 1 has been done for you.

MERRY MISCHIEF

Spot Wally, Woof (you can only see his tail), Wenda, Wizard Whitebeard, Odlaw and their lost things below. Then hide ten present stickers in the scene for your friends to find.

WALLY'S KEY

WOOF'S BONE

WENDA'S CAMERA

WIZARD WHITEBEARD'S SCROLL

ODLAW'S BINOCULARS

MORE THINGS TO FIND

- A Santa giving flowers to a fairy
- A pile of square snowballs
- A Santa with his hat over his face
- A Santa showing off
- An upside-down Santa
- A Santa skiing up hill
- A broken ladder
- An angry snowman

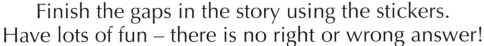

WIZARD WHITEBEARD AND THE CHUCKLE CURSE

Finish the gaps in the story using the stickers.
Have lots of fun – there is no right or wrong answer!

Once upon a time a stole the smiles from everyone in the

land with a bah-humbug curse. A wise was summoned to

create a jolly spell, but he needed three ingredients before he could

begin. He set off in search of a who gave him a .

Next he visited a who showed him where to

find a . Then, a guided him through a

prickly pine forest (ouch!) to meet a , Keeper of the .

At last, the wizard had gathered all he needed. He waved his

magic and boomed Ho-Ho-Cadabra! The curse was broken

and everyone laughed happily ever after!  **THE END**

DANCING ON ICE

SANTA'S SACK RACE MAZE

DEAR SANTA

SNOWBALL SPLAT!

WENDA'S CLEVER CLOGS QUIZ

HOME SWEET HOME

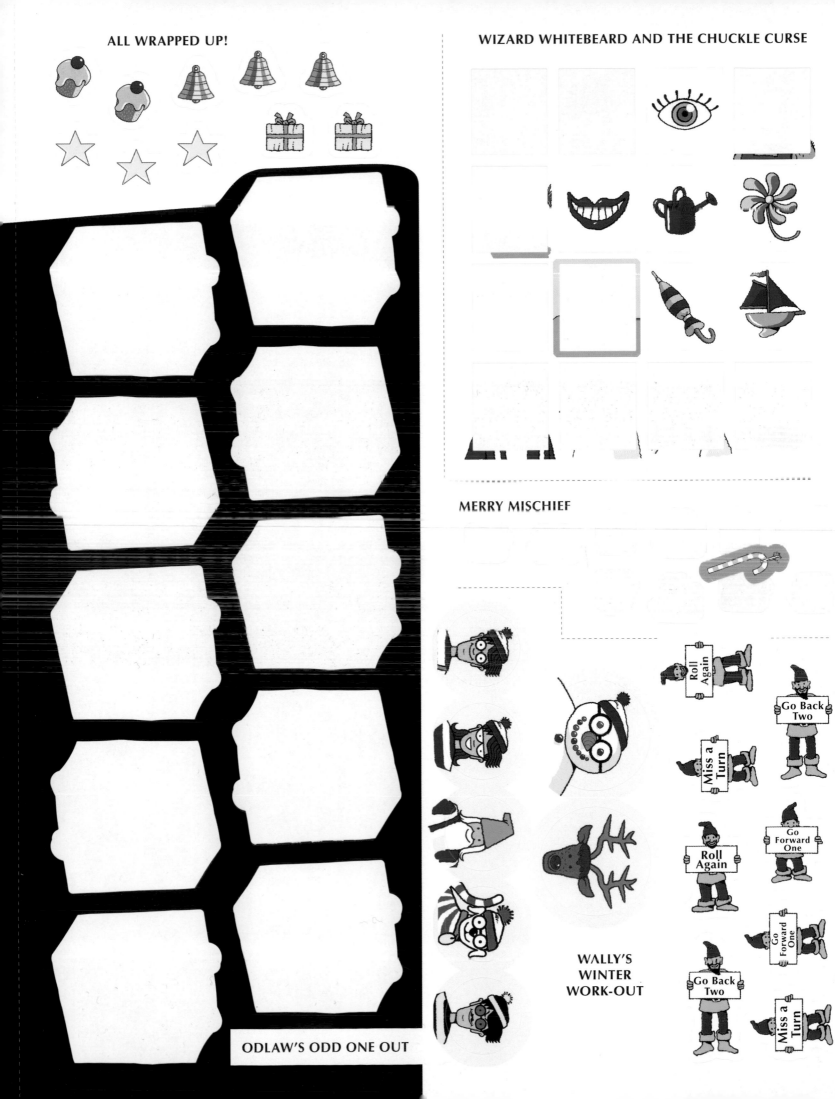

ALL WRAPPED UP!

WIZARD WHITEBEARD AND THE CHUCKLE CURSE

MERRY MISCHIEF

ODLAW'S ODD ONE OUT

WALLY'S WINTER WORK-OUT

Roll Again

Go Back Two

Miss a Turn

Roll Again

Go Forward One

Go Forward One

Go Back Two

Miss a Turn

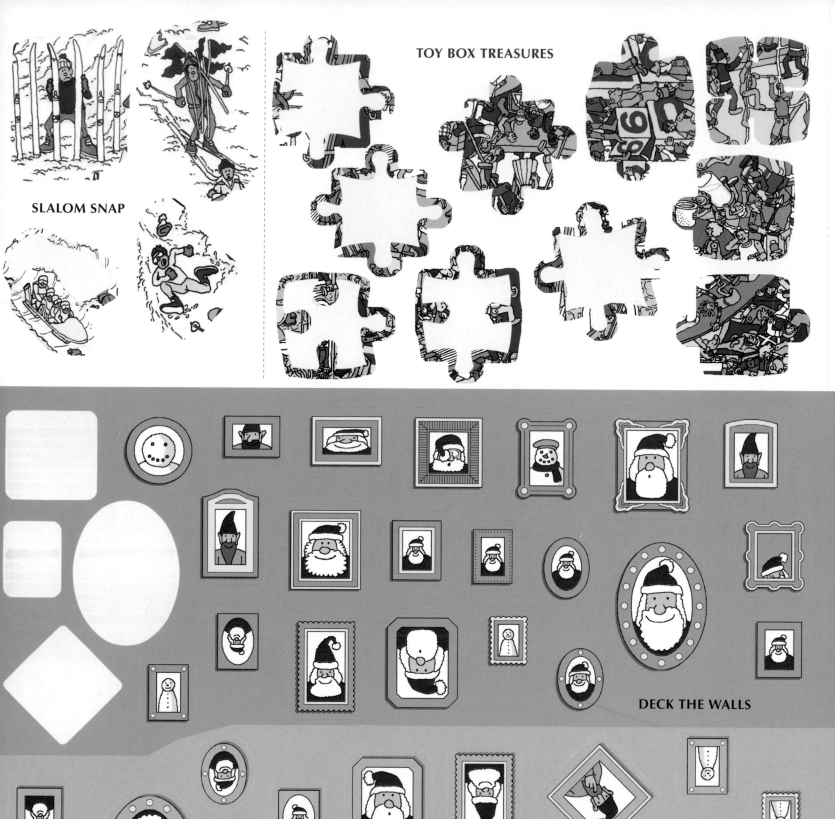

SLALOM SNAP

TOY BOX TREASURES

DECK THE WALLS

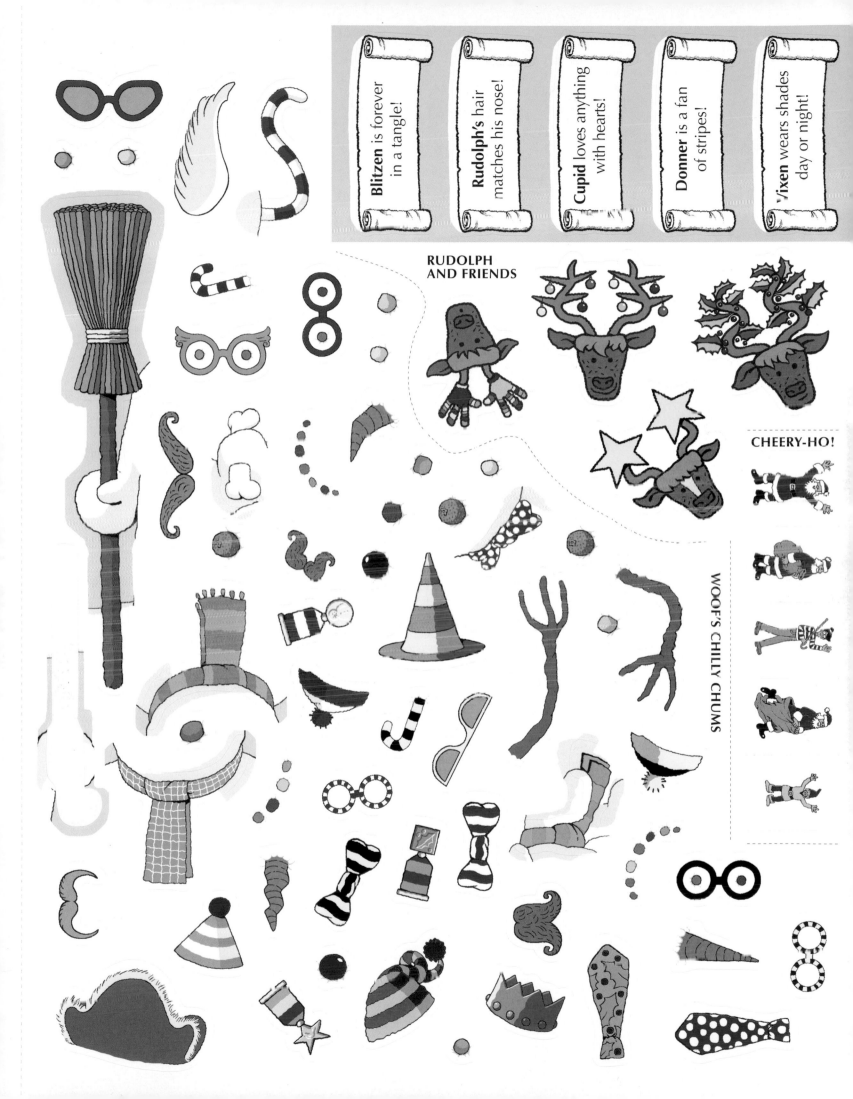

RUDOLPH AND FRIENDS

CHEERY-HO!

WOOF'S CHILLY CHUMS

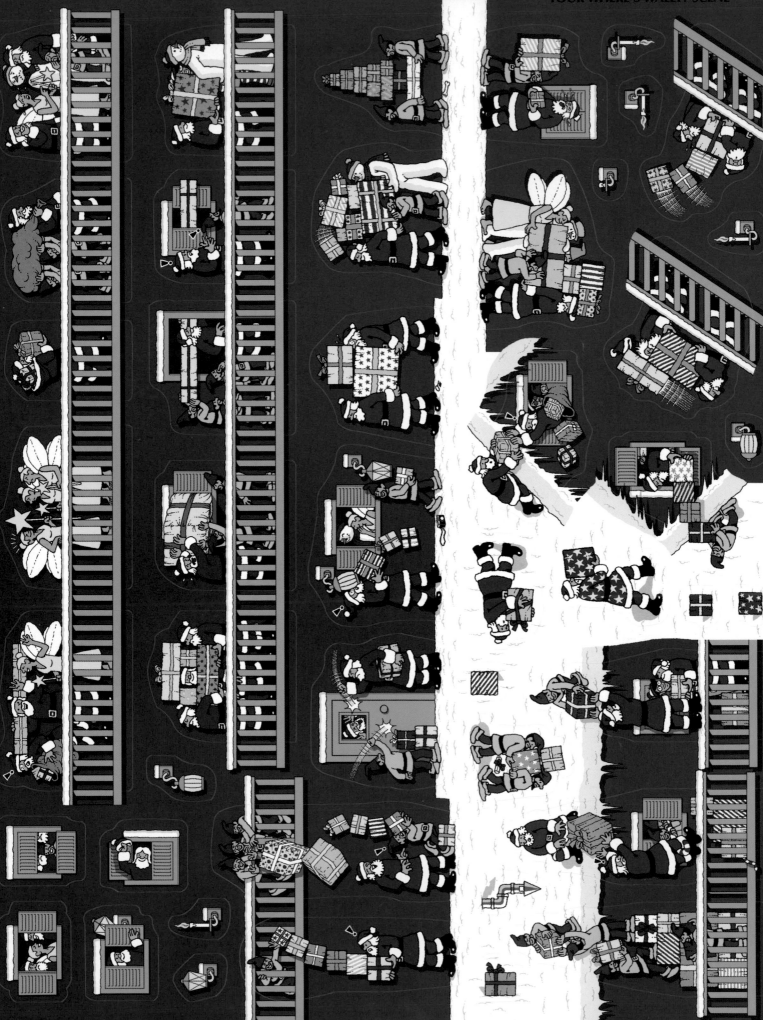

ODLAW'S ODD ONE OUT

Read the riddles and use the present stickers to cover the items that each riddle rules out. Which gift is left unwrapped?

* Wrap me if I'm delicious to eat…
* Or if I have wheels or feet…
* Or if I beat or blow a tune…
* Or if I have spots…
* And if I can float.

What am I?

1 START

2 Repeat "Ho Ho Ho" until your next go!

3

4 URDOLHP
Clue: Bright red nose

UNSCRAMBLE THE LETTERS AND ADD THE STICKER.

5

8 Find five candy canes then roll again!

9

10 Hop until your next go. Boing! Boing!

11 Pretend to be a polar bear. Grrr!

12

15 Full steam ahead! Find another one of these:

16 Describe Wally without saying Wally.

17

18 Tell this joke: *What do snowmen eat in their sandwiches?*

Iceberg lettuce

19

22 Mime an elf getting dressed!

23 Pretend to stamp snow off your boots! Stomp! Stomp!

24

25 Count eight stars.

26

32

33

34 Find another one of these:

35 Run around the room three times. Phew!

36

42 Do a skiing mime. Swoosh! Swoosh!

43

44

45 Find three spotty presents.

46

WALLY'S WINTER WORK-OUT!

How to play the game:

✱ Find up to five players and a die.

✱ Stick the character stickers to card to make a counter for each player.

✱ Add the forfeit stickers where you like on the board.

✱ Place the counters on START and take it in turns to roll the die to move, completing the activities on the board as you go.

✱ If you land on your character square, move forward five spaces.

✱ The first person to FINISH wins!

6

7 Draw a snowman in the air!

13

14 Hum a Christmas tune. Tra-la-la!

20

21 Find eleven Santas.

27

28 Find another one of these:

29 UNSCRAMBLE THE LETTERS AND ADD THE STICKER. NOMWASN *Clue: A cool character*

30 Find another one of these:

31 Say "Santas Sing Silly Songs" five times!

37

38 Do your best Santa laugh. Tee hee!

39 Go back two. Boo! Hiss!

40

41 Send everyone back to their character square. Bah-humbug!

47

48 Find five Christmas stockings.

49 Make a wish for your favourite present!

50 FINISH

SLALOM SNAP

Find four almost-matching pairs. Then finish the scenes with the stickers to make them identical.

MORE THINGS TO DO

* Photocopy the page at least twice and cut out the cards to play a game of snap with your friends.

* Can you find a character in these pictures that appears in the scene on the 'Snowball Splat!' activity?

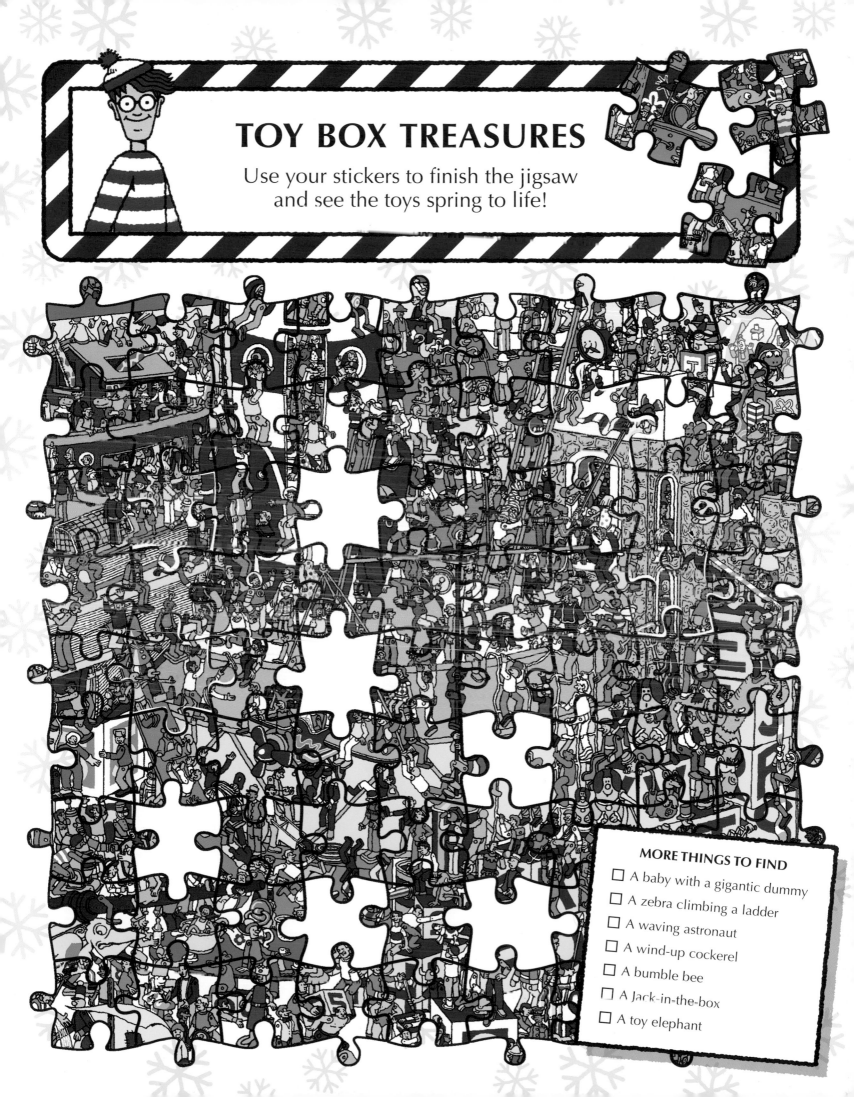

TOY BOX TREASURES

Use your stickers to finish the jigsaw
and see the toys spring to life!

MORE THINGS TO FIND

☐ A baby with a gigantic dummy

☐ A zebra climbing a ladder

☐ A waving astronaut

☐ A wind-up cockerel

☐ A bumble bee

☐ A Jack-in-the-box

☐ A toy elephant

DECK THE WALLS

Hang the blue-framed portrait stickers on the blue wall and the green-framed ones on the green wall.

Now spot ten differences between the two sets of portrait pictures. Test your friends too!

One last thing! Study the border of the golden frames to find the odd Santa out.

MORE THINGS TO FIND
- Sunglasses with red frames
- Two green umbrellas
- Two men wearing blue braces
- A man wearing an orange suit
- A man wearing a green jumper
- A woman wearing a spotted skirt
- A man wearing green dungarees

MORE THINGS TO DO

✳ Give your snowmen
(and snowdog!) names.

✳ Draw snowmen
outlines on paper,
then doodle on them
or dress them with
any leftover stickers.

✳ Write a snowman
tongue-twister!

WOOF'S CHILLY CHUMS

Have fun dressing Woof's fabulously frosty friends before they thaw out!

RUDOLPH AND FRIENDS

Pair each reindeer to its name by sticking down either a reindeer picture or a scroll in the spaces.

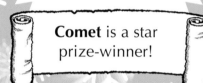

Comet is a star prize-winner!

Dancer adores flashing lights!

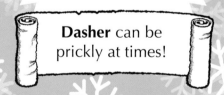

Dasher can be prickly at times!

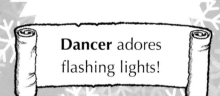

Prancer keeps his antlers toasty!

CHEERY-HO!

Study the picture sequences from left to right
and place the correct sticker in the gaps.

MORE THINGS TO FIND

☐ Six elves on shoulders

☐ An elf with yellow boots

☐ A Santa without a belt

☐ A sleigh

☐ Six Santas with hooded coats

☐ An elf poking fun

WELL DONE, WINTER WANDERERS!
I HOPE YOU HAD A SPARKLING TIME COMPLETING THE PUZZLES. DID YOU FIND THE REAL SANTA WITH A MISSING BOOT (HE'S WEARING A STRIPY SOCK)? AND DID YOU SEE ME DRESSED AS SANTA? HO, HO, HO!

I FOUND THESE TAGS WITH OUR NAMES ON THEM. LOOK THROUGH THE BOOK TO FIND OUR MATCHING WRAPPED PRESENTS.

WALLY   WOOF   WENDA   WIZARD WHITEBEARD   ODLAW

A MERRY TREAT IS IN STORE FOR YOU NOW! OPEN THE FLAP AND CREATE YOUR OWN SCENE WITH ME AND MY FRIENDS. HAVE FUN!

Wally

Can you find these pictures in the book?

Answers

Santa's Sack Race Maze: The Santa in the red sack passed the most presents.

Dear Santa: Wally – A globe; Woof – A bone; Wenda – A pair of scissors, a pencil and notepaper; Wizard Whitebeard – A pair of slippers; Odlaw – A joke spider; The Snowman – An ice cream.

Wenda's Clever Clogs Quiz: From left to right: The Arctic; A calf; 31 days; Green all year round; Swim; A sledge; Jingle Bells; Six points.

Odlaw's Odd One Out: The rocket is the odd one out.

GAME 2

GAME 3

GAME 4

All Wrapped Up!

Rudolph and Friends
Donner
Prancer
Vixen
Dancer
Blitzen
Dasher
Rudolph
Comet
Cupid

Cheery-Ho!